Lucky
Socks

For Jack, my inspiration
C.W.

For my parents, my sister, Endaf and Daniel,
for their continuing support and endless patience
C.M.

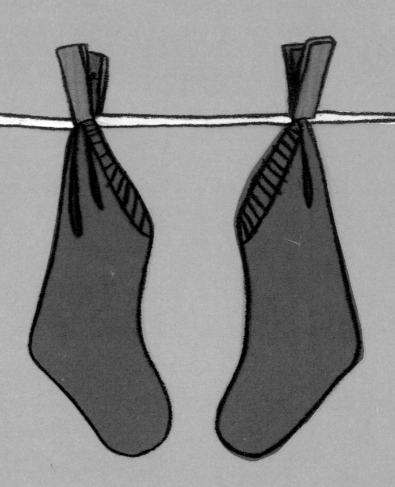

First published in the United States 2002 by
Phyllis Fogelman Books
An imprint of Penguin Putnam Books for Young Readers
345 Hudson Street
New York, New York 10014
Published in Great Britain 2001 by
Gullane Children's Books

1 3 5 7 9 10 8 6 4 2

Library of Congress Cataloging-in-Publication Data
available upon request.

120-7418

Lucky Socks

Carrie Weston

Illustrated by

Charlotte Middleton

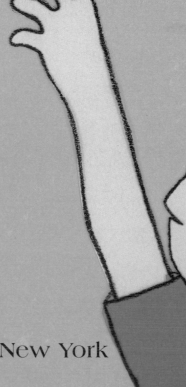

Phyllis Fogelman Books New York

On Monday morning
Kevin put on his red socks.

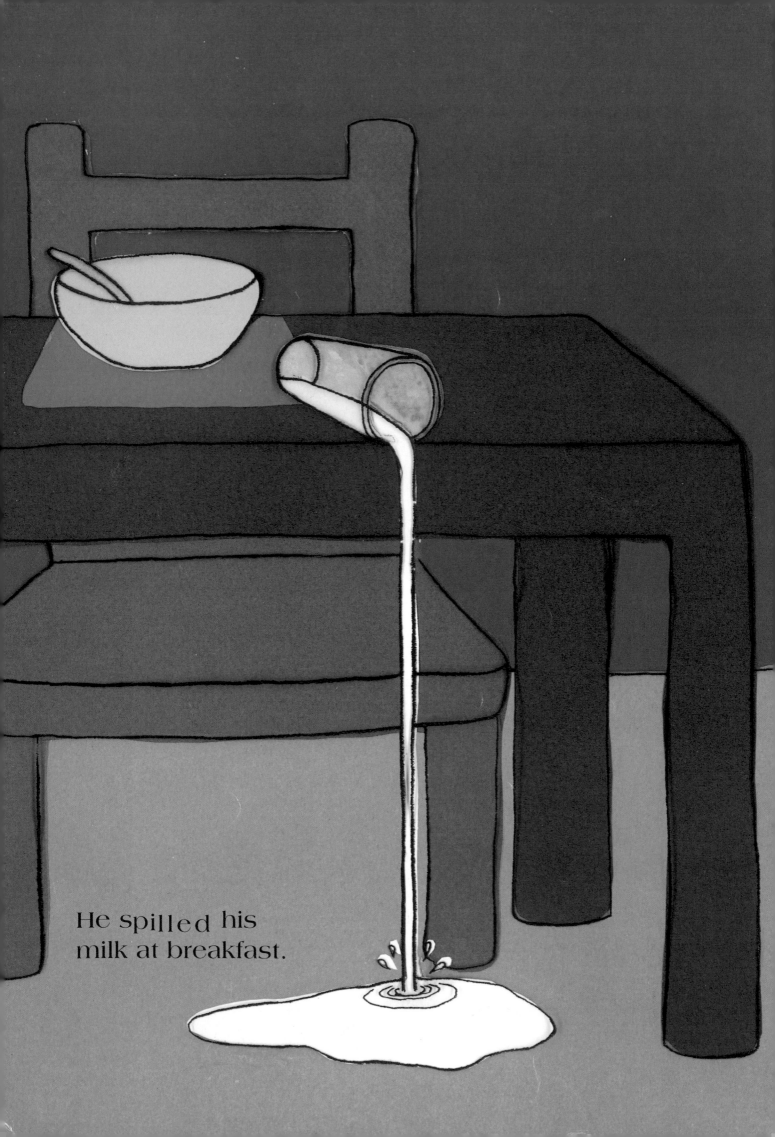

He spilled his
milk at breakfast.

The button

p o p p e d

off his shorts.

And he was late for school.

On Tuesday Kevin
wore his green socks.
He got his spelling
all wrong at school.

And his bicycle got a f l a t.

On Wednesday Kevin wore his blue socks. It rained all day . . . and he dropped his sticker collection.

On Thursday
Kevin wore
his striped
socks . . .

and his beetle escaped from his
bug jar.

There wasn't
enough time
for Kevin to
take his turn on
the computer . . .

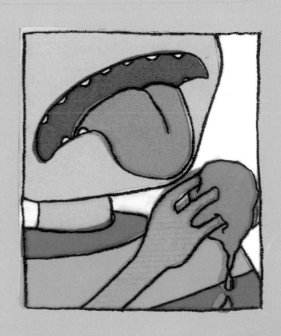

and it was meat
loaf surprise for
lunch.

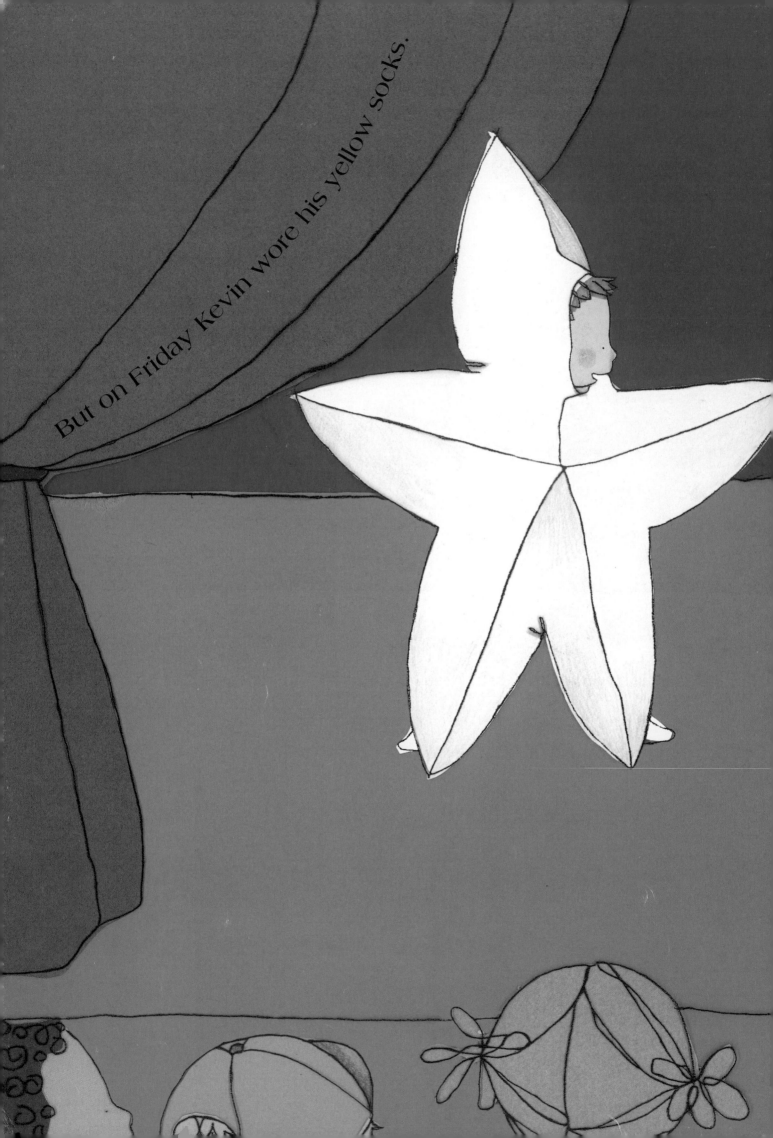

But on Friday Kevin wore his yellow socks.

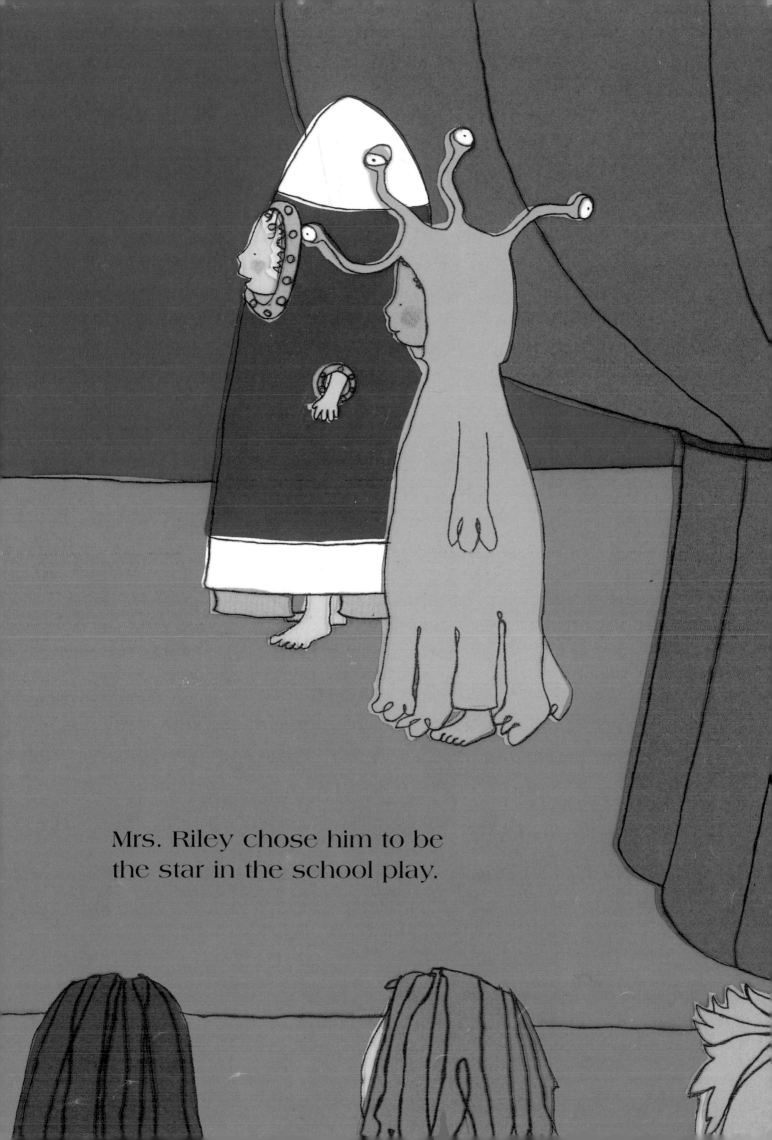

Mrs. Riley chose him to be
the star in the school play.

The next time Kevin
wore his yellow socks,
Billy Bennet invited him over
to his house to build a tent.
They found ice cream
in the freezer.

Whenever Kevin had his yellow socks on,
his writing always seemed to fit on the page.

Yesterday I went to Billy's howse.
We had ize creem and bilt a tent.
Then we looked for bugz in the garden.
I fownd tow worms and a sentipeed.
Billy fownd a big spider. It waz
all hary. We put the bugz in Billys
bug jar. Billy sed it wud be a nice
surprise for his mom and dad. We
put the bug jar on the table at
snack time. Billy waz rite. His mom
and dad wer very suprised. <u>By Kevin.</u>

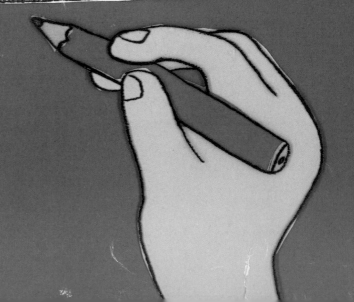

Kevin's ball never went
over the fence when he
wore his yellow socks, and
he never ever went home
with muddy knees.

But on the morning of
field day at school,
Kevin couldn't find
his yellow socks.

He looked in
the drawer.

He looked in
the closet.

He looked
under his bed.

He looked in his bed.

He looked through
the dirty laundry.

He even looked
in the fridge.

Kevin's mom helped him look.
She found some red socks, blue socks,
some gray socks, polka dot socks,
tiger-stripe socks, fire engine socks,
and even Kevin's old baby socks.
  "I need my yellow socks!" wailed Kevin.

All his mom could find were
some old yellow underpants.

Kevin was unhappy
all the way to school.
He was unhappy as he
got changed for field day.

Then Kevin fell
flat on his face
in the sack race.

He got all mixed up
in the dress-up race.

And he just couldn't balance his beanbag

in the balance-the-beanbag-on-your-head race.

Kevin thought about
his yellow socks as the
other children went up
to get their medals.

Then Mrs. Riley called
out Kevin's name. . . .

Kevin got a special medal.
It was for trying very hard at
everything—and never giving up!
Everyone cheered and clapped for Kevin.
He felt really proud.

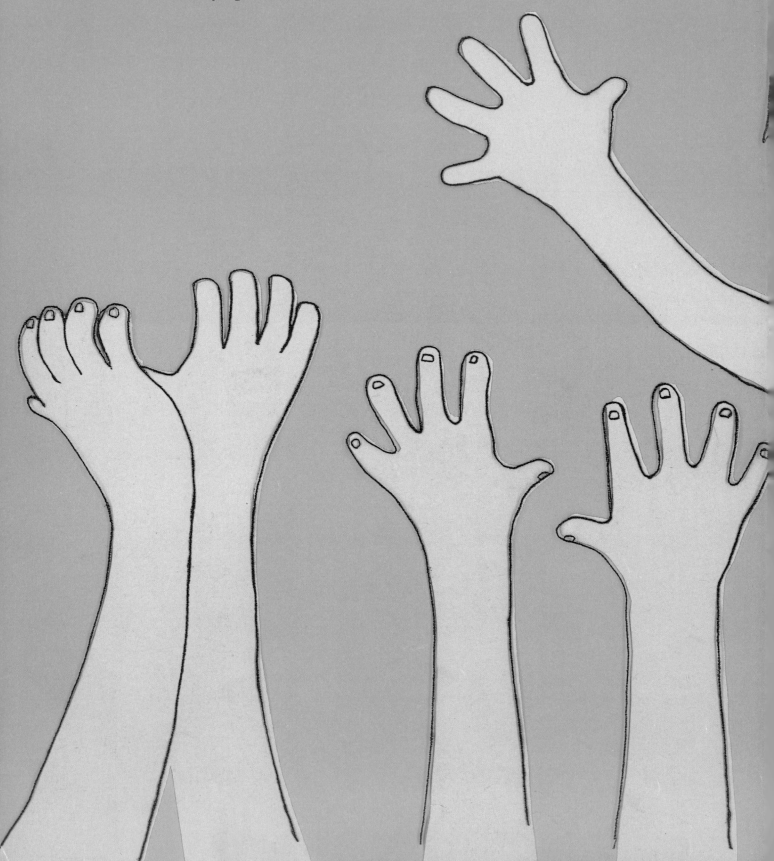

Now Kevin doesn't
mind what color
socks he wears . . .

But he's very fond of his yellow underpants!

3/26/02

05/02   1   05/02

4/11	47	9/10
11/16	55	4/16
1/19	55	—
10/20	55	—

BAKER & TAYLOR